Copyright © Text and Illustrations Colin & Jacqui Hawkins 1991

The rights of Colin and Jacqui Hawkins to be identified as the
author and illustrator of this work have been asserted by them
in accordance with the Copyright, Designs and Patents Act, 1988.

Designed by Alison Fenton
Handlettered by Alan Dempsey

First published in 1991 by The Bodley Head Children's Books
an imprint of The Random Century Group Ltd
20 Vauxhall Bridge Road, London SW1V 2SA

Printed in Hong Kong

British Library Cataloguing in Publication Data is available.

ISBN 0 370 31508 1

NUMBER THREE

Written and illustrated by
Colin & Jacqui Hawkins

The Bodley Head
London

"It's wonderful being me," said Number Three, "but I can't remember why!" He lived in a little red house with three blue chimney pots and three yellow windows at 3, Number Lane, Numbertown, NT3.

Number Three had three umbrellas to make sure he never got wet. He also saved all his pocket money in three fat, pink, piggy-banks.

In his bedroom there were three large toyboxes but, most important of all, there were three alarm clocks as Number Three always forgot the time.

One day, while Number Three was out shopping it rained and rained and rained.

"I am a drip," said Number Three. "I forgot my umbrella." He got very wet and sneezed, "Atishoo! Atishoo! Atishoo!" Number Three wheezed off to bed.

"I don't feel well," he sniffed miserably.

After three days in bed, Number Three felt a lot better. He got up and had a long, hot shower. He used three bars of soap and three bottles of shampoo.

"Squeak, squeak, squeak. I'm squeaky clean now," he bubbled happily.

Number Three was eating his breakfast, when there was a loud knock at the door.

"It's the post," he said, as three letters popped through the letterbox. Number Three quickly tore them open.

"It's my birthday," he said in surprise. "Happy Birthday to me!"

"I'll make a birthday cake," said Number Three, "and invite my friends for tea."

He found a recipe for a special chocolate cake. "I'm a whizz at this," said Number Three as he whisked, whipped and whirled.

"Now, have I forgotten anything?" he said peering into his store cupboard.

"Yummy, that's scrummy," said Number Three. He poured the cake mix into three round cake tins and popped them into the hot oven. Three hours later Number Three sniffed the air.

"Sniff, sniff, sniff. What's cooking? Oh no! My cakes!" he cried. He rushed to the oven but it was too late. The cakes were all black and burnt.

"I'll have to go and buy a birthday cake," said Number Three. So he hopped on his scooter and three minutes later he was whizzing past Numbertown Park.

"That looks fun," said Number Three looking at the swings. "I must have a go!"

Number Three had a wonderful time playing on the swings. "I can fly!" he cried swinging through the air.

Then he had three long rides on the roundabout. "I feel dizzy," he giggled as he wobbled towards the slide.

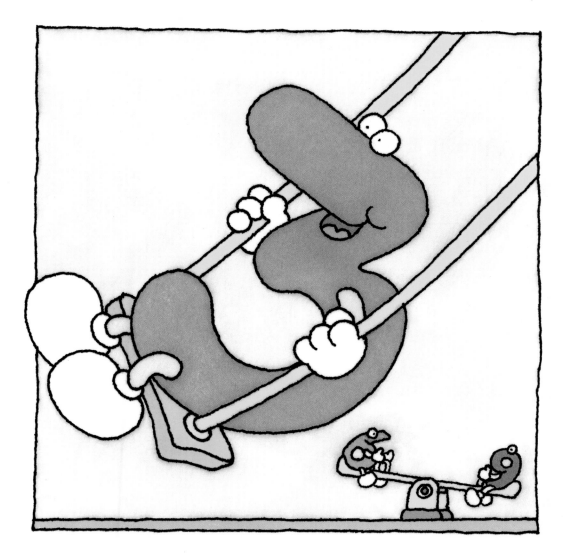

"Whee!" whooped Number Three as he swooped down the slide. Up and down he went, over and over again.

"Look at me!" he shouted. Number Three was having such fun that he forgot all about the time.

Bong! Bong! Bong! chimed the Numbertown clock.

"Oh no, it's three o'clock," said Number Three. "I've forgotten my cake." He jumped on his scooter and sped to the cake shop, but it was closed.

"Oh, crumbs!" said Number Three. "What shall I do now?"

Then sadly, he pushed off towards home.

I must get the cake

"I forget everything," sighed Number Three as he pushed open the door.

"Happy Birthday!" shouted Numberlies One and Two. They gave Number Three a big birthday cake and three presents. He blew out the candles and wished three wishes.

"How old are you?" asked Number One as they all tucked into the cake.

"I've forgotten," said Number Three, and they all hooted with laughter.